RUMPEL-STILTSKIN

RETOLD BY
DOROTHY JOAN HARRIS

ILLUSTRATED BY
REGOLO RICCI

TORONTO OXFORD NEW YORK
OXFORD UNIVERSITY PRESS
1991

For Zachary Michael
—D.J.H.

For Anna
—R.R.

There was once, long ago and far away, a country ruled by a very wise young King. Despite his great wealth and power, King Harold was modest and hated all boasting.

Now, one hot day when the King was out riding, he stopped for a drink of water at a poor miller's house. The miller had very little, but he was a terrible braggart.

As King Harold drank the cool well-water, he noticed the miller's daughter feeding their few scrawny goats. His heart skipped a beat for he could see at once how kind and gentle she was. "Your daughter is very lovely, with her long golden hair," he remarked.

"Ah!" cried the miller, eager to impress his King. "That is not all that is golden about Elinore. She has always been as good as gold. And she has a golden voice—sweet enough to charm the birds from the trees. And..." the miller paused to think of something truly amazing to say about his daughter, "...why, she is so clever that she could even spin this barnyard straw into gold!"

The King was offended by these boastful words.

"Indeed?" he said coldly, deciding to teach this braggart a lesson. "This I must see. Bring your daughter to the palace today." And he rode off.

Immediately, the miller regretted his silly boast. But it was too late. With heavy hearts, he and his golden-haired daughter set out for the palace.

Now, the King never meant to harm the miller's daughter in any way, but he did intend to teach her father a lesson. So Elinore was taken to a high tower room with nothing in it but a stool, a spinning wheel and a pile of straw. And after the door was locked behind her the King turned to the miller and said, "Unless she can spin this straw into gold by morning, your daughter shall not return home again."

When darkness fell the miller's daughter, sitting alone and helpless, began to weep bitterly. Then, as the church clock struck midnight, she felt an icy wind about her and before her very eyes a strange little man seemed to pass right through the locked door.

She stared in amazement at him, and at his bushy, red beard and his dark, glittering eyes. "Who are you?" she asked. "How did you get through that door?"

The little man cackled. "That I will not tell you," he replied.

"Then, why have you come?"

"I heard you weeping. And I know why you weep. You have been commanded to spin this straw into gold."

The girl nodded sadly. "That is true, but I don't know how to do such a thing." She looked through her tears at the strange little man. "Please, can you help me?"

"Perhaps, if the reward is right. What will you give me if I do?"

"I have nothing of much value, but I could give you this," said Elinore, undoing the simple necklace her mother had given her.

The little man snatched the necklace and put it on. "Agreed!" he said, and sat himself down at the spinning wheel.

Elinore watched in astonishment as the little man reached for a bundle of straw and began to spin. He turned the wheel three times: *whirr, whirr, whirr,* and the bobbin was full of fine, spun gold!

The man worked all night until the straw was gone and in its place lay many spools of gold thread. And then, as daylight crept into the tower room, he slipped back through the locked door and vanished.

A short time later the key turned in the lock and there in the doorway stood the King with the frightened miller.

The King was amazed when he saw the spools of fine, spun gold. But when he looked at Elinore sitting quietly on the stool, he saw only her tear-stained face. He regretted the worry he had caused her, but alas, before he could say anything the miller burst forth.

"There now!" cried the miller, swallowing his own surprise. "See how clever my daughter is! And she could do as much and more, any time she wishes."

Now, King Harold already had all the gold he needed, so it wasn't greed that made him do what he did next. It was the miller's renewed boasting. Apparently this foolish man hadn't learned his lesson yet.

"Indeed?" he said, "Then have her do as much again and more, if you wish to take your daughter home. Bring more straw!" he ordered. And turning from the sight of the horrified girl he strode off, taking the miller with him.

When the servants had brought an even larger pile of straw the miller's daughter sank down on it in despair. She lay there all day and well into the night. But then, as midnight struck, she felt the icy wind once more, and in through the locked door came the strange little man.

"Aha!" he crowed. "And what will you give me this time to spin straw into gold?"

Elinore took a thin small ring from her finger. "Well," she said slowly, "I could give you my grandmother's ring."

The little man quickly put it on his finger. "Agreed!" he said and sat down at the spinning wheel again.

W*hirr, whirr, whirr,* went the wheel all night long, until the pile of straw had been spun into gold. Then, at daybreak, the little man vanished. A short time later the King, with the miller beside him, appeared in the doorway.

Once more the King stared in wonderment at the gold on the floor. And once more his heart went out to the weary girl whose eyes were red from weeping. But once more, too, the foolish miller began to brag.

"You see, my King, how clever she is? And she could do even more..."

"More straw!" King Harold shouted, interrupting the miller. But when he looked into Elinore's frightened eyes, he wished he could have taken back his order. He wouldn't keep her there against her will, but he couldn't bear to send her home. For now he realized he loved her with all his heart.

"Elinore," he said gently, "this is the last time for such an order. Tomorrow, if this too is turned into gold, you may go if you wish. But I would be the happiest man alive if you would stay and become my Queen."

That day, as the miller's daughter sat surrounded by piles of straw, she wondered about the King's proposal. And she wondered what would happen if the strange little man did not come again. But he did, right on the stroke of midnight, as usual.

"Aha!" he exclaimed, rubbing his hands together. "And what will you give me this time?"

"I have nothing left to give," the girl answered sadly.

"You may have nothing now—but when you are Queen, you will have much to give. And then I shall want your first child."

The girl was astonished. "How could you know what the King said to me, up here in this high tower?"

"That I will not tell you. But can you really believe," he scoffed, "that a King would marry a lowly miller's daughter?"

Elinore hung her head. "Perhaps not," she murmured.

"Of course not," jeered the little man. "He's simply playing games with you. You might as well agree to my terms. There will never be a child, so what have you got to lose?" And without waiting for a reply, he sat himself down and began to spin.

Now the girl was deeply troubled. She was afraid of making such a promise to this strange little man, but she was just as afraid not to. So she sat in silence as he worked, saying neither yes or no.

By dawn, the little man had vanished and the floor of the room was covered with spools of gleaming gold. And that morning, true to his word and deeply in love, King Harold asked Elinore to marry him. And, wonder of wonders, on that morning too, the miller finally found the wits to keep his mouth closed, though his eyes bulged wide at the effort of keeping his pride to himself.

It wasn't long before Elinore grew to love King Harold and in time they were married. Their happiness was complete when, a year later, a beautiful son was born to them.

But with the birth of her child, the Queen began to worry. From time to time she remembered the promise the little man had demanded, and how she had agreed to it with her silence.

Now it happened that the King had to make a journey to another country and would be gone for some time. And it was while he was away that one evening, as the shadows were creeping in, the strange little man appeared in the Queen's room.

He stood before her and fixed his glittery eyes on her. "Now you must give me what you promised," he told her, pointing at the little prince in her arms.

Elinore shrank back in horror and tightened her arms around her son. "No, not my baby," she pleaded. "Look, I will give you this fine necklace and this heavy gold ring instead. They are much more valuable than the ones I gave you before."

"No," said the little man, shaking his head firmly.

"Then I will open the treasury and give you all the gold that you spun," she offered.

"No," he said, shaking his head again.

"Then," wept the Queen, "I will give anything—do anything, if only you will go away."

"There is only one way to get rid of me," he taunted, "and that is to call me by name."

Elinore looked through her tears. "Call you by name? Will that make you go away?"

"It will!" announced the little man. "And just to be fair, I will give you three days in which to do it." And then he vanished as suddenly as he had appeared.

Straightaway, Queen Elinore called her servants to her and bade them go out through the kingdom to collect and bring her all the names they could find. They obeyed their Queen without question and returned the following day with a huge list for her.

That evening when the little man appeared in her room, Elinore began to read every name on the list.

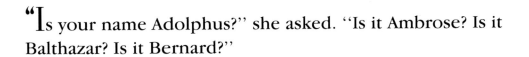

"Is your name Adolphus?" she asked. "Is it Ambrose? Is it Balthazar? Is it Bernard?"

But to each name the little man answered gleefully, "No, no, no." And when she was finished he danced twice around the infant's cradle. "Two more days," he warned and then vanished as before.

Again, the Queen sent for her servants. "Ask everyone you meet for every name they have ever heard, no matter how strange," she said.

They came back the next day with an even longer list, and when the little man appeared that night, the Queen started to read feverishly.

"Is your name Spindleshanks?" she asked. "Or is it Bandylegs? Could it be Gobbledegook?"

But to every name the little man shook his head. "No!" he squealed triumphantly. "None of those names is mine." Then he pranced once around the baby's cradle and warned, "One more day!" before he vanished.

Now the Queen was in despair. But this time her father, who had come to see his grandson, found her weeping. Upon hearing the whole story, he was determined to help her. After all, it was his boasting that had put the child in danger.

"There is one place in the kingdom where I'll wager no one has searched," he told her, "and that is the dark forest country at the farthest edge of the land. I will take a fast horse and go there to see what names I can find."

"No one dares go near those dark forests," said Elinore.

"Nevertheless I will," said the miller. And to prove his words, he rode off immediately.

All the next day the Queen waited anxiously for her father to return. Not till the sun was just about to set did he ride wearily through the palace gates.

Elinore hastened to meet him. "What did you find in those dark forests?" she asked.

"I found a place where the trees grow so thickly together that sunlight never reaches the ground. And then, as I pushed through the branches, I came upon a clearing and I saw your small, red-bearded man, dancing around a fire and singing to himself."

"Quickly, father, what was he singing?" the Queen asked eagerly.

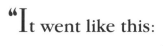"It went like this:

> *My spell is done, the child is won,*
> *The prince is mine 'ere set of sun.*
> *None can now prevent my claim,*
> *For Rumpelstiltskin is my name!''*

With that, the overjoyed young mother clapped her hands and hugged her father. She hurried to her room and when dusk fell and the red-bearded man appeared, Queen Elinore was waiting.

"Now then, oh Queen," said the evil little man, "your time is up. Tonight you must guess my name or give me your son."

Elinore sat very still and pretended to think hard. "Is it... Hans?" she asked timidly.

"No!" he answered, edging toward the cradle.

"Is it ... Hubert?"

"No!" he said again with a wicked gleam in his eyes.

"Then, how about...is it perhaps...could it possibly be... *Rumpelstiltskin*?"

With that the little man flew into a terrible rage. He shrieked and screamed and stamped his feet in fury. "It was the devil who told you that!" he screeched.

He stamped so hard, first with one foot and then the other, that he split the ground open and stamped himself right down into the earth. Then the ground closed over him, and Rumpelstiltskin was never seen in that country again.

As for King Harold and the miller's daughter, the story ended happily after all. The King never knew what had taken place while he was away, for Elinore and her father agreed it should be their secret.

And the miller? Why, he never boasted or bragged again, unless of course, it was about his grandson. But that, even the King had to allow, since anyone could plainly see that the yellow-haired boy was as good as — no, better than — gold.